MW01119001

Dedicated to my favorite little person. I am so proud of your bravery. You are the source of my inspiration.

Parent Introduction

Welcome to the second book in the "Where Hands Go" series!

This book is intended to start meaningful conversations between children and their caretakers about body safety. The first book in this series, "Where Hands Go," presented a gentle introduction to inappropriate or uncomfortable touch to children. This book builds on that foundation by teaching them ten body safety rules they can keep in their minds and hearts while at school.

If you are reading this book to your child, please note that some words within the text may be difficult for young children to understand and require explanation. Consider reviewing the facts, definitions, and resources in the back of this book before reading it with your child.

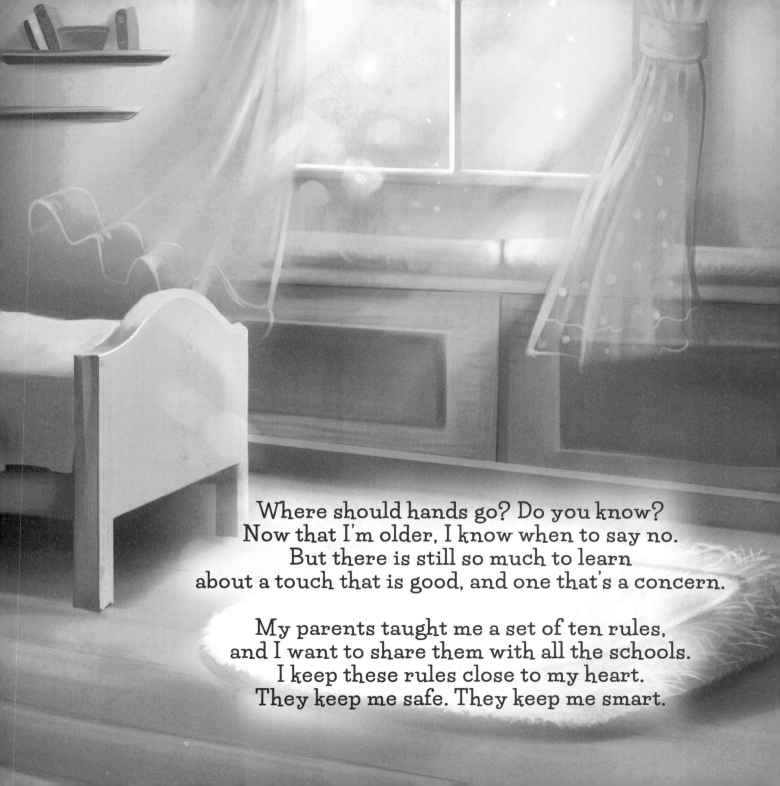

Where should hands go? Do you know?
Now that I'm older, I know when to say no.
But there is still so much to learn
about a touch that is good, and one that's a concern.

My parents taught me a set of ten rules,
and I want to share them with all the schools.
I keep these rules close to my heart.
They keep me safe. They keep me smart.

I remember rule number one when I'm in doubt.
Here is what it's all about.

#1) You are the boss of your own body.
It doesn't belong to anybody.
If you don't want to be touched,
you have the right to say no.
Then, you can get up and off you'll go.

Rule number two is to remind you and me,
that parts of our bodies are not for others to see.

#2) Our bodies need our love and care.
They're not something we have to share.

Rule number three might not be fun and games,
but it's okay, let me explain.

#3) Games should not involve kissing
or touching private parts.
They're called private for a reason,
so always trust your heart.

Shh, it's time to tell some secrets.
Here's rule number four.
Don't worry if you've never said it before.

#4) Never hide a secret that makes
you worried, upset, or hurt.
And don't be afraid to raise an alert.
True feelings should never be hidden,
especially when actions are forbidden.

Rule number five is all about others.
We should look out for each other, like sisters and brothers.

#5) Touching someone else's body parts is not okay,
and you have the right to run away.

No matter the time, place, or event,
Rule number six is all about consent.

#6) Always say no to being touched and kissed,
even when they try to resist.
Your body is precious and so is mine.
Not hugging and kissing is completely fine.

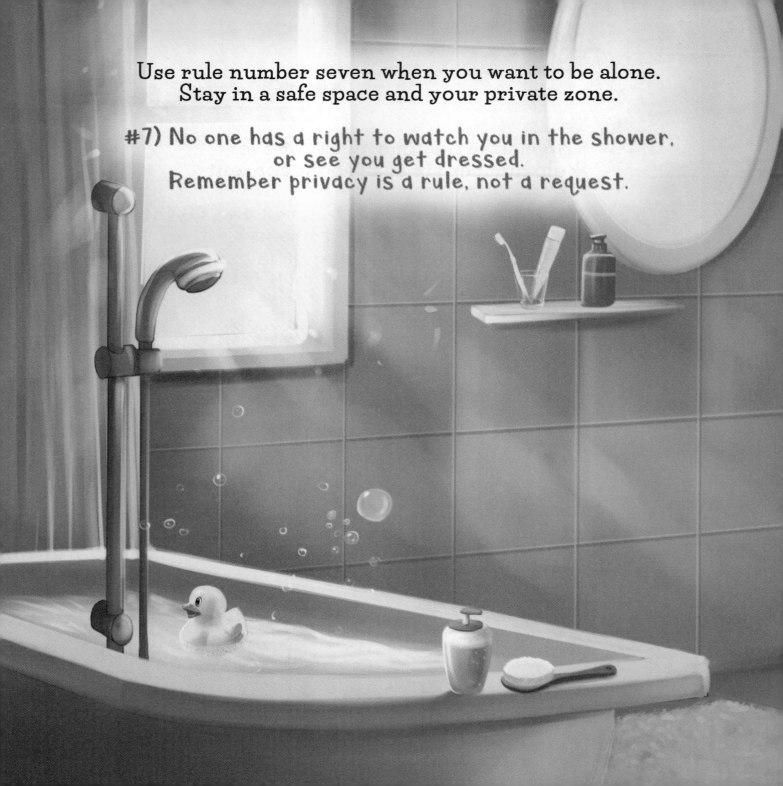

Use rule number seven when you want to be alone.
Stay in a safe space and your private zone.

#7) No one has a right to watch you in the shower,
or see you get dressed.
Remember privacy is a rule, not a request.

If you feel unsafe, use rule number eight.
And don't feel like you have to wait.

#8) Feelings are important. Don't keep them inside.
If something feels wrong, you shouldn't have to hide.

Rule number nine is about knowing who to trust.
Speaking to someone you love is always a must.

#9) Always speak to someone trustworthy
either family or a friend
and it will all be fine in the end.

Last but not least, here's rule number ten.
Repeat these rules again and again.

#10) Hands can be gentle. Hands can be kind.
But if they're not, then speak your mind.

Use these rules wherever you go.
Your power is in what you know.

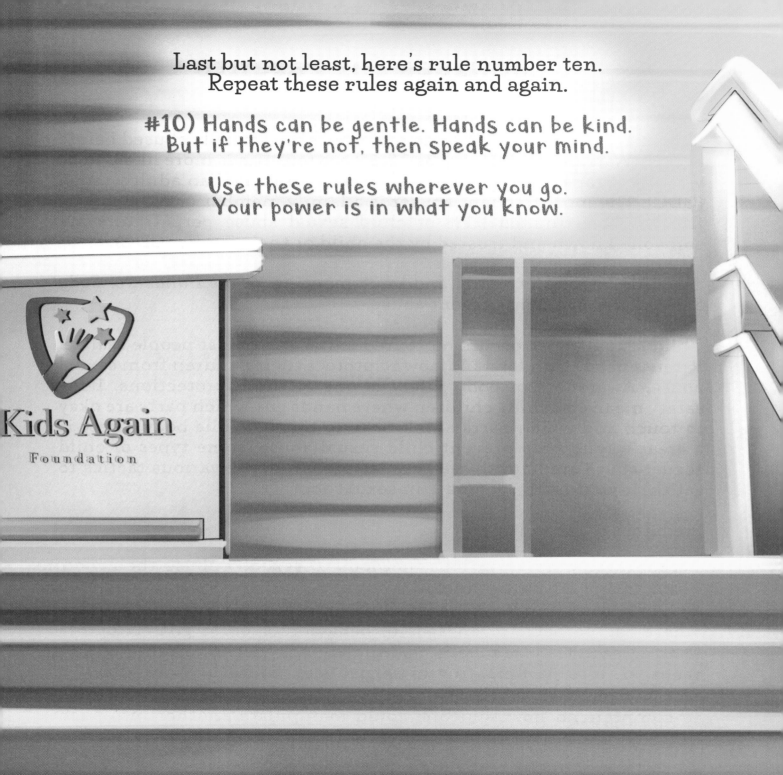

Resources For Parents

One in every four girls and one in six boys are sexually abused before age 18 (Warrior). Children ages 12-17 are four times more likely to be victims of rape, attempted rape, or sexual assault than adult women (CDC). The most frequent abuser is a family member or close family friend. An estimated 91% of child sexual abuse perpetrators are someone known and trusted by the child or their family (CDC).

Teaching body safety early and implementing *Where Hands Go: Body Safety Rules* can help prevent abuse.

Child sexual abuse occurs more frequently than most people realize. Parents need to understand how to protect their children from sexual abuse. Awareness of body safety is one of those protections. Body safety means teaching children where hands go—which parts are okay to touch and which parts aren't okay to touch. While body safety is a great way to help prevent child sexual abuse, some types of child sexual abuse are hard to see because predators use various tactics to get their victims to cooperate in sexual acts.

Predators & Grooming

Perpetrators employ various methods to sexually abuse their victims, often taking advantage of the trust and familiarity established with their victims. This is achieved through a process known as grooming, where the perpetrator engages in behaviors such as gift-giving or sharing secrets to gradually manipulate the victim, often a child or teenager, into participating in sexual acts. Unfortunately, these tactics can be so subtle that they go unnoticed, making it challenging to comprehend how someone could manipulate another into such a personal and intimate act.

This makes it even more critical for parents and caregivers to talk with children about body safety early on—and continue talking about it throughout childhood and adolescence.

Gift Giving: The perpetrator may give gifts or money to the victim in exchange for sexual favors.

Sharing Secrets: The perpetrator may share secrets with the victim to make them feel special and grown-up, then use this information later to threaten the victim, so they don't tell anyone what happened.

It can be hard for parents and caregivers to discuss sexual abuse prevention with their children. Nevertheless, this does not mean there aren't ways to talk about it that help kids learn how important it is for them to protect themselves from abuse. The most important thing is for parents and caregivers to begin talking about body safety early on—and continue talking about it throughout childhood and adolescence.

Where Does Child Sexual Abuse Happen?

Studies show that 91% of child sexual abuse happens at home, not in public places or on the street. Teach your children about body safety and keep them safe. Let them know that it is never okay if someone tries to touch their genitals or get them to touch another person's genitals, and it should be reported immediately. If a child ever tells you they have been sexually abused, always believe them.

How Can I Help My Child?

While children need to learn body safety rules and recognize potentially dangerous situations, adults ultimately must protect children. As a parent, you are your child's most important role model. The most effective way to protect against sexual abuse is through education. All children have the right to be protected from sexual abuse. It is the responsibility of adults to educate themselves about the warning signs, prevention efforts, and responsibilities for reporting. Knowledge is power!

Be available to listen whenever your child wants to talk. Let your child know that you are there for them, will support them, and believe what they tell you.

How Can We Teach Our Kids to Protect Themselves?

Many parents are very aware of their child's physical surroundings but may not know about keeping their child safe from sexual abusers. By teaching our children about body safety and practicing these skills with them, we can empower them to protect themselves against these actions and report any harmful situations they are a part of. One way you can help your child learn body safety is by using open-ended questions during your everyday conversations. This will allow you to find out what your child already knows about body safety and also provide an opportunity for you to teach new information or reinforce what they already know. Here are some examples of open-ended questions that you could ask your child:

● What would you do if someone tried to touch or kiss you in a way that made you feel uncomfortable?
● Whom should you tell if someone tries to touch or kiss you?
● If someone tries to touch or kiss you, what should you do?
● What are the ten body safety rules?
● Why do you think it is important to learn these rules?

Another important thing to remember when teaching body safety is not to blame or shame your child. Your goal as a parent should be to empower them with the knowledge to protect themselves against any harmful situations they may encounter. You don't want them feeling afraid or ashamed of their bodies because these feelings may prevent them from reporting any harmful situations they experience. Instead, use positive language to let them know it isn't their fault if something happens. It's never okay for anyone else to touch their private parts without permission! Also, remember that body safety applies not only to sexual and physical abuse.

What If I Think My Child Has Been Sexually Abused?

If you think your child has been sexually abused, acting quickly is essential. Notify authorities and get your child help. The National Center for Missing & Exploited Children (NCMEC) recommends four steps to take when you suspect a child has been sexually abused: report, preserve, investigate, and protect. Report — Call 911 or your local police department immediately. You may also contact a Child Advocacy Center or another victim assistance program in your area for guidance.

References

Arata, C. (2002). Child sexual abuse and sexual revictimization. Clinical Psychology Science and Practice, 9, 135-164.

(Centers for Disease Control and Prevention [CDC], 2014). Subsequent citations: (CDC, 2014). https://www.kuow.org/stories/this-is-nothing-like-stranger-danger-one-man-s-story-of-the-scourge-of-child-sexual-abuse

Cloitre, M., & Rosenberg, A. (2006). Sexual revictimization: Risk factors and prevention. In V. M. Follette & J. I. Ruzek (Eds.), *Cognitive-behavioral therapies for trauma* (pp. 321-361). New York, NY: Guilford.

Fergusson, D. M., Horwood, L. J., & Lynskey, M. T. (1997). Childhood sexual abuse, adolescent sexual behaviors and sexual revictimization. *Child Abuse & Neglect*, 21, 789-803.

Felitti, V. J., Anda, R. F., Nordenberg, D., ... & Marks, J. S. (1998). Relationship of childhood abuse and household dysfunction to many of the leading causes of death in adults: The Adverse Childhood Experiences (ACE) study. *American Journal of Preventive Medicine*, 14, 245-258.

Finkelhor D, Shattuck A, Turner HA, Hamby SL. The lifetime prevalence of child sexual abuse and sexual assault assessed in late adolescence. J Adolesc Health. 2014 Sep;55(3):329-33. doi: 10.1016/j.jadohealth.2013.12.026. Epub 2014 Feb 25. PMID: 24582321

Finkelhor, D., & Shattuck, A. (2012). Characteristics of crimes against juveniles. Durham, NH: Crimes Against Children Research Center.

Retrieved from http://www.unh.edu/ccrc/pdf/CV26_Revised%20 Characteristics%20 of%20Crimes%20against%20Juveniles_5-2-12.pdf

"Google and Microsoft Catch People Sending Images of Child Abuse." Computer Act!Ve, no. 430, Dennis Publishing Ltd., Aug. 2014, p. 7.

Leeb, R. T., Lewis, T., & Zolotor, A. J. (2011). A review of physical and mental health consequences of child abuse and neglect and implications for practice. *American Journal of Lifestyle Medicine*, 5, 454-68.

Letourneau, E. J., Brown, D. S., Fang, X., Hassan, A., & Mercy, J. A. (2018). The economic burden of child sexual abuse in the United States. *Child Abuse & Neglect*, 79, 413-422.

Merrick MT, Ford DC, Ports KA, Guinn AS, Chen J, Klevens J, Ottley P. Vital Signs: Estimated Proportion of Adult Health Problems Attributable to Adverse Childhood Experiences and Implications for Prevention—25 States, 2015-2017. *Morbidity and Mortality Weekly Report* 2019; 68(44), 999.

Mosack, K. E., Randolph, M. E., Dickson-Gomez, J., Abbott, M., Smith, E., & Weeks, M. R. (2010). Sexual risk-taking among high-risk urban women with and without histories of childhood sexual abuse: mediating effects of contextual factors. Journal of child sexual abuse, 19(1), 43-61. https://doi.org/10.1080/10538710903485591

Norman RE, Byambaa M, De R, Butchart A, Scott J, et al. (2012) The Long-Term Health Consequences of Child Physical Abuse, Emotional Abuse, and Neglect: A Systematic Review and Meta-Analysis. PLOS Medicine 9(11): e1001349. https://doi.org/10.1371/journal.pmed.1001349

Ogloff, J., Cutajar, M., Mann, E., & Mullen, P. (2012). Child sexual abuse and subsequent offending and victimisation: A 45 year follow-up study. Trends & issues in crime and criminal justice no. 440. Canberra: Australian Institute of Criminology.

Bebbington, P. E., Cooper, C., Minot, S., Brugha, T. S., Jenkins, R., Meltzer, H., & Dennis, M. (2009). Suicide attempts, gender, and sexual abuse: Data from the 2000 British Psychiatric Morbidity Survey. *American Journal of Psychiatry*, 166, 1135-1140.

Putnam, F. W. (2003). Ten-year research update review: Child sexual abuse. *Journal of the American Academy of Child & Adolescent Psychiatry*, 42, 269-278.

Tang S, Ports KA, Zhang K, Lin HC. Adverse childhood experiences, internalizing/externalizing symptoms, and associate prescription opioid misuse: A mediation analysis. *Prev Med*. 2020 May; 134. doi:10.106/j.ypmed.2020.106034.

Traumatic events and children: MedlinePlus Medical Encyclopedia. https://medlineplus.gov/ency/patientinstructions/000588.htm

Warrior Within: Healing Childhood Abuse. Book 1 How Trauma Effects the Brain, Personal Values & Affirming Self-Worth https://books.apple.com/ie/book/warrior-within-healing-childhood-abuse-book-1-how-trauma/id1542853795

What should I do if I think my child has an intellectual and developmental disability (IDD)? https://www.nichd.nih.gov/health/topics/idds/conditioninfo/cure

Whitfield, C. L., Anda, R. F., Dube, S. R., & Felitti, V. J. (2003). Violent childhood experiences and the risk of intimate partner violence in adults: Assessment in a large health maintenance organization. *Journal of Interpersonal Violence*, 18, 166-185.

Widom, C.S. & Massey, C. (2015). A prospective examination of whether childhood sexual abuse predicts subsequent sexual offending. JAMA Pediatr. 169(1):e143357

World Health Organization. (2003). *Guidelines for medico-legal care for victims of sexual violence*. Geneva, Switzerland: Author.

About the Author

Krystaelynne is an author and child sexual abuse advocate dedicated to using her writing to educate and empower children. With a background in criminal justice, political science, and ethnic studies, she has made it her mission to prevent child sexual abuse and promote positive self-esteem in young readers. As a mother, Krystaelynne is passionate about providing children with the tools they need to develop confidence and strength in facing life's challenges. In her work as an advocate, she is committed to positively impacting children's lives. Krystaelynne currently resides in Northern California with her husband and son, who provide her with love and support in her work as an advocate.

In addition to her books, Krystaelynne offers bulk discounts, school visits, and resources on child sexual abuse prevention. To learn more and stay updated, visit her website and follow her on social media.

Website: **www.ksdiggs.com**
Email: **author@ksdiggs.com**
Instagram: **@allthingsdiggs**
Facebook: **Author K Sanders Diggs**
Scan for Important Links >>>